The Girls FC series

*Do Goalkeepers Wear Tiaras?*

*Can Ponies Take Penalties?*

*Are All Brothers Foul?*

*Is An Own Goal Bad?*

*Who Ate All The Pies?*

*What's Ukrainian For Football?*

*So What If I Hog the Ball?*

*Can't I Just Kick It?*

*We're the Dream Team, Right?*

**Helena Pielichaty** (pronounced Pierre-li-hatty) has written numerous books for children, including *Simone's Letters*, which was nominated for the Carnegie Medal, and the popular After School Club series. A long-standing Huddersfield Town supporter, there are few who could write with as much enthusiasm about girls' football. A local girls' under 11s team helps with the inspiration and tactical know-how, but Helena has been an avid fan of women's football for many years. It clearly runs in the family: her aunt was in a women's team in the 1950s and her daughter has been playing since she was ten (she is now twenty-six!). Helena lives in Nottinghamshire with her husband and has two grown-up children.

# We're the Dream Team, Right?

**Helena Pielichaty**

WALKER
BOOKS

For Hanya: awesome footballer, awesome

daughter

This is a work of fiction. Names, characters, places and incidents
are either the product of the author's imagination or, if real,
used fictitiously. All statements, activities, stunts, descriptions,
information and material of any other kind contained herein are
included for entertainment purposes only and should not be
relied on for accuracy or replicated as they may result in injury.

First published 2011 by Walker Books Ltd
87 Vauxhall Walk, London SE11 5HJ

10 9 8 7 6 5 4 3 2 1

Text © 2011 Helena Pielichaty
Cover illustration © 2011 Sonia Leong

The right of Helena Pielichaty to be identified as author
of this work has been asserted by her in accordance with
the Copyright, Designs and Patents Act 1988

This book has been typeset in Helvetica and Handwriter

Printed and bound in Great Britain by Clays Ltd, St Ives plc

British Library Cataloguing in Publication Data:
a catalogue record for this book is available from the British Library

ISBN 978-1-4063-1741-1

www.walker.co.uk

# ☆ ☆ The Team ☆ ☆

☆ **Megan "Meggo" Fawcett** GOAL

☆ **Petra "Wardy" Ward** DEFENCE

☆ **Lucy "Goose" Skidmore** DEFENCE

☆ **Dylan "Dyl" or "Psycho 1" McNeil** LEFT WING

☆ **Holly "Hols" or "Wonder" Woolcock** DEFENCE

☆ **Veronika "Nika" Kozak** MIDFIELD

☆ **Jenny-Jane "JJ" or "Hoggy" Bayliss** MIDFIELD

☆ **Gemma "Hursty" or "Mod" Hurst** MIDFIELD

☆ **Eve "Akka" Akboh** STRIKER

☆ **Tabinda "Tabby" or "Tabs" Shah** STRIKER/MIDFIELD

☆ **Daisy "Dayz" or "Psycho 2" McNeil** RIGHT WING

☆ **Amy "Minto" or "Lil Posh" Minter** VARIOUS

**Official name:** Parrs Under 11s, also known as the Parsnips

**Ground:** Lornton FC, Low Road, Lornton

**Capacity:** 500

**Affiliated to:** the Nettie Honeyball Women's League junior division

**Sponsors:** Sweet Peas Garden Centre, Mowborough

**Club colours:** red and white; red shirts with white sleeves, white shorts, red socks with white trim

**Coach:** Hannah Preston

**Assistant coach:** Katie Regan

# ☆ ☆ Star Player ☆ ☆

☆ **Age:** 10

☆ **Birthday:** I'd rather not say, if you don't mind

☆ **School:** a prep school somewhere in Leicestershire

☆ **Position in team:** central midfield

☆ **Likes:** the usual stuff

☆ **Dislikes:** answering personal questions like this! Sorry.

☆ **Supports:** England, England Women

☆ **Favourite player(s) on team:** they're all great

☆ **Best football moment:** they're all the best

# Gemma "Hursty" Hurst

☆ **Match preparation:** none, really. I tend to play down the football side of things at home, so I don't make a big deal out of it in the house.

☆ **Have you got a lucky mascot or a ritual you have to do before or after a match?** No – unless waiting for Amy to sort her hair out counts.

☆ **What do you do in your spare time?** I just hang out with my friends.

☆ **Favourite book(s):** no comment

☆ **Favourite band(s):** no comment

☆ **Favourite film:** no comment

☆ **Favourite TV programme(s):** no comment

# Pre-match Interview

Hello, my name is Gemma Hurst and I ~~play~~ used to play in the Parrs U11s football team. I played central midfield. It's January when I start my piece and freezing cold. The weather forecasters had predicted the worst winter in years, but we had somehow managed to play all our matches so far.

As you can see from the league table (over the page), the Parrs were doing well - but we'd lost in a top-of-the-table clash to the Furnston Diamonds mid-week, so they'd pulled ahead. Our biggest rivals, Grove Belles, had an easy match over Lutton Ash Angels to become joint leaders with the Diamonds. And that's it. Sorry if you were expecting something more personal. I'm not good at that kind

of thing. Writing this has been a
real challenge for me and I only
agreed because I'd promised Megan
and I don't like letting people
down...

Anyway, here it is. My story.

Thank you for taking the time to
read it.


Gemma

# The Nettie Honeyball Women's Football League junior division

| Team | P | W | D | L | Pts |
|------|---|---|---|---|-----|
| Furnston Diamonds | 9 | 6 | 2 | 1 | 20 |
| Grove Belles | 9 | 6 | 2 | 1 | 20 |
| Parrs U11s | 9 | 5 | 2 | 2 | 17 |
| Greenbow United Girls | 9 | 4 | 4 | 1 | 16 |
| Tembridge Vixens | 9 | 3 | 4 | 2 | 13 |
| Hixton Lees Juniors | 9 | 3 | 2 | 4 | 11 |
| Cuddlethorpe Tigers | 9 | 3 | 1 | 5 | 10 |
| Misslecott Goldstars | 9 | 2 | 1 | 6 | 7 |
| Southfields Athletics | 9 | 2 | 0 | 7 | 6 |
| Lutton Ash Angels | 9 | 1 | 1 | 7 | 4 |

# 1

**I'll begin at after-school club because that's where it all started to unravel.** It was a Thursday, half four-ish. Amy and I were trying to revise in the book corner. Mrs Rose, the supervisor, had done a great job of fencing us off from the rest of the kids, but she couldn't prevent Eve from slipping through the blockade of beanbags. "Come on, you guys," Eve had begged us. "I've got homework, too."

We wouldn't have minded but Eve's homework seemed to be to talk all the time. "Guess what? Frank Lampard called round to our house last night," she said.

"That's nice," Amy mumbled.

"Really nice," I added.

"He stayed for ages, drinking tea, eating Jaffa

Cakes, having a laugh. Mum asked him to go in the end because she wanted to watch *MasterChef*."

"That's nice," Amy mumbled again.

"Really nice," I added again.

"Yeah," Eve replied. "It was. And guess what else? Before he left he gave me three tickets for the Chelsea–Liverpool game. He told me to bring my two closest friends."

"Nice."

"Really nice."

"Pity that's both of you out, then."

"What's that supposed to mean?" Amy asked, her voice rising several decibels.

Eve, head down, arms sprawled across the desk, let out a low groan. "It means I'm so fed up of you two ignoring me that I'm being forced into having imaginary conversations with myself!"

"No, I mean *that*," Amy said and slid her revision sheet across to me. "'Underline the compound words.' What in the name of Gok Wan's glasses is a 'compound' word?"

"Amy! Miss Sturgeon did compound words with us this morning!" I reminded her.

"You know I don't hear anything Miss Sturgeon says. I get too distracted by her horrendous cardigans."

"Miss Sturgeon? You've got a teacher called Miss *Sturgeon*?" Eve laughed.

Amy glowered. "Yes? So?"

"So it's a funny name."

"Not really."

Eve turned to me. "Hey, Gemma. Has your dad ever caught a sturgeon on one of his fishing trips?"

I tensed at the unexpected mention of my dad. "What? I don't know. Maybe."

"What's the biggest fish he's ever caught?"

"Erm…" I stalled, glancing at Amy for help.

It came immediately. "Eve, babes, no offence, but would you mind butting out so we can revise in peace? This *is* meant to be the quiet corner."

Eve scraped her chair back and stood up. "Sure. No probs. I'll go mingle with the other common people not going to a posh school next year."

"Thank you," said Amy sweetly.

I raised my eyes to the ceiling. Sometimes Amy's help didn't help at all.

As Eve headed for the beanbags, I signalled to Amy to make amends. "Hang on, Akky," she said, and I relaxed, thinking she was going to apologize. "I need to tell you something."

"What?" Eve asked, one leg halfway over the beanbags.

"My mum can't do the lifts to football on Saturday."

Eve twisted back round, a scowl on her face. "Well, mine can't either. She's got to drive Claude and Sam to their match in Leicester or Loughborough or Lapland or somewhere in the total opposite direction of Cuddlethorpe."

I felt just as put out as Eve. It was the first I'd heard of it, too, and I'd been at school with Amy all day. "What? How come?" I said.

Amy's hand swept over her books. "Er ... hello ... revising!"

"But it's only at Cuddlethorpe. We'll be finished by lunchtime."

"Exactly. That's half a day lost."

"But I need you," I said.

"No you don't. It's football. You never need me at football."

"I do!"

"You don't. Parties, yes. Classrooms, yes. Football, no."

"But, Amy…"

"She's right; you don't need her," Eve agreed, suddenly at my side, her arm resting on my shoulder. "Not when you've got me around."

I continued to look pleadingly at Amy. Amy was my faithful bodyguard, always on hand to step in and protect me. She'd been doing it since we were six and I saw no reason for her to stop now. I tried another tack. "But my mum's really busy. She has to get to the showroom early. It's the January sales…"

*"Hurst's Modern Kitchens of Mowborough.*

*Today's modern kitchens made to yesterday's highest standards,"* Eve trilled.

I cringed. The jingle was bad enough when it was played on the local radio. Hearing it here made me want to dive under the table. "Please come, Amy."

"Gem, I'm not a brainiac like you. If I don't revise I won't pass the entrance exam, and if I don't pass the entrance exam you'll end up sitting with Portia Poohsbreath and that lot at St Agatha's. Is that what you want?"

I shuddered. Portia and her gang were dreadful. "No."

"Then stop hassling me."

I groaned. "Mum's going to be so cross."

"What about your dad? Can't he drop us off?" Eve asked.

"He'll be fishing," Amy and I automatically chorused.

"Even in winter?"

"Especially in winter. It's an all-year-round sport."

"Couldn't he go later? Just for once?"

"It's OK, it's OK. Mum'll do it," I offered quickly, to prevent the bad feeling spreading. "She won't mind."

"Cool," Eve said, heading back to the beanbags. "See you Saturday, partner."

"And I'll see you Monday," Amy called.

"Whatever," Eve replied. "Which, by the way, is a compound word."

# 2

**As predicted, Mum wasn't impressed about being volunteered to do the run.**

"What? But I picked up from training on Tuesday," she groaned as she dropped down a gear to climb Toft's Hill.

"Sorry," I said. "Amy wants to revise and Eve's mum is going the other way."

"Fine. Add it to the list."

"Sorry," I repeated.

Mum frowned at me in the rear-view mirror. "We really do need to talk about Saturdays, Gemma."

I shuddered at the thought. "I'll buy you a bar of Galaxy when I get my pocket money," I told her hastily.

She caught my anxious tone and sighed. "I'll hold

you to that, though I reckon it's Amy who should be buying it, not you."

"Too right," I agreed. "Giant size."

A minute later we were entering Castle Heights. Castle Heights is a gated complex of seven large, mock-Georgian, detached houses, all set back from each other in a sweeping semicircle. As Mum tapped the code into the keypad by the wrought-iron gates and waited for them to open, I focused on our house: smack in the middle, proudly overlooking the communal oval of grass. I couldn't help smiling. I was home, safe and sound.

"I hope your dad's made dinner. I'm starving," Mum said, parking behind Dad's SUV.

"Me too," I told her.

As soon as our footsteps triggered the outside security lighting, the front door opened. Caspar and Jake, our two Border collies, bounded out and started leaping and yelping and going bonkers, like they always do when we come home. I giggled as Jake tried to lick my face.

"Kriss!" Mum called out, pushing Caspar away from her suit.

Dad appeared, his arms out wide, his dreadlocks framing his beaming face. "Come to poppa, girls!" he greeted. The dogs, presuming he meant them, turned and leapt on him, but he shooed them inside and held out his arms for Mum and me. I giggled again. Dad looked so daft dressed only in his T-shirt, shorts and bare feet.

"Dad! It's minus three!"

"So? I can deal wid a li'l cold snap, y'know what I'm saying?" he boasted, putting on what he thought was a Caribbean accent.

"I can't," Mum said with a shrug, heading inside.

The house was roasting. No wonder Dad was in shorts.

"The gas bill's going to be enormous!" Mum tutted, turning down the thermostat in the hall on her way to the kitchen.

"You see, you try to make the home nice and cosy

for the missus and the kids when they get back and what happens? Immediate grief," Dad complained. He winked at me.

"Speaking of immediate grief, where's Lizzie?" Mum asked, glancing around the kitchen. Lizzie is my sister. She's seventeen, at college, has green hair, about three trillion Facebook friends and, despite working weekends in the showroom, is always broke.

"Ellie's," Dad said, going to stir something on the hob. A delicious aroma of spices filled the air. My dad's a great cook.

"Did she say what time she'd be back?"

"Nope. Why? Is there a problem?"

"Nothing major. I wanted to talk to her about Saturday."

"Saturday?" Dad asked.

"I need her to cover for me while I drop Gemma off at Cuddlethorpe. Problems with lifts, as per."

"For football, you mean?"

"Yes," Mum said. They exchanged that special

little look I wasn't meant to see and my stomach clenched.

Dad took a sip from the spoon, then said casually, "I'm free Saturday. I could do it."

"No thanks, Dad," I replied quickly. "Mum's on it." I plucked an apple from the fruit bowl and headed upstairs, pretending not to notice Mum's resigned shrug and the hurt in my dad's eyes. Amy, you owe me, I thought as I threw my uniform on my bed. You owe me big time.

# 3

**Saturday morning was bitterly cold.** My breath puffed out ahead of me like a vintage steam train as I hurried down the tiled path leading to the Akbohs' terraced house. At the porch I swivelled my arms and hips from side to side to keep warm, taking care not to knock into the brightly coloured plant pots full of herbs, while I waited. I knew Eve had seen me, so I didn't knock – she'd waved from her bedroom window as we'd pulled up outside.

Seconds later she was there, beaming at me. "Nice day for it, Hursty," she said, ramming a woolly hat with earflaps over her head. "I know I look geeky, but I don't care. It's better than having icicles for ears."

"Totally."

"I don't know how your dad can go fishing in this

weather. I hope he's got his thermals on."

"He has. Double lots. Did you lock the door?"
I asked, so the topic could change before we got
into the car. Mum gets more wound up than me if
she has to discuss Dad's fishing trips. Luckily, Eve's
conversation usually leaps about like a frog bouncing
from one lily pad to another.

"Course I did. Wotcha, Mrs H.," she greeted Mum
as she climbed into the back seat. "Cold, innit?"

"Hello, Eve." Mum smiled.

"Thanks for the lift."

"You're welcome. I've been compensated." She
patted the bar of Galaxy on the seat next to her.

"Nice." Eve grinned. "But for future reference, you
should go for a Bounty. It counts as one of your five
a day. Coconut, see?"

"Good tip." Mum laughed.

Eve nodded gravely. "I know my chocolate."


When we arrived at the ground it felt even colder
than when we'd set off. As soon as I stepped out of

the car, my face felt like a freshly baked loaf being slid into a freezer.

"OK, then, girls?" Mum said as she leaned across to give me a kiss.

"Thanks again for bringing us, Mrs Hurst," Eve said.

"No worries. And your mum's OK to drop Gemma back at the shop?"

"Defo. She might even be back in time for our second half."

"Just give me a shout if there's any problem."

"Will do."

"Good luck."

"We don't need luck," Eve said, clamping her arm around my shoulder. "Not when the Parrs have got the Dynamic Duo."

"'Dynamic duo'?" I said to Eve as Mum drove off and we made our way towards the playing fields.

"Too Batman-ish?"

"A little."

"The Terrific Two? The Perfect Pair? The Dream Team?"

I was almost glad Amy wasn't here. She would have been making gagging noises by now. "Erm…"

Eve's eyes lit up. "That's the one: the Dream Team, because that's what we are when we play, aren't we?"

"If you say so."

"I so say so!" She laughed.

We reported to Hannah, our coach, and Katie, the assistant coach, on the touchline. "What a relief to see you two," Hannah said, marking us off. She glanced around. "No Amy?"

"Revising."

Hannah hit her forehead with her clipboard. "What are you lot trying to do to me?"

"You're dropping like flies," Katie told us.

It turned out that nearly half the squad was missing. Holly had a bad cold, the twins couldn't make it because it was their gran's seventieth birthday and Nika had an eye infection.

"Well, the good news is you all get sixty minutes!" Hannah said. "Best get warmed up before you all freeze to death."

So off we went, jogging round the perimeter of the pitch in a ragged line. Jenny-Jane, Tabinda and Lucy were to my left. Eve was on my right with Megan and Petra alongside her.

"Hey, Hursty?" Megan said.

"Yes?"

"Is it next week you're off because of that exam thing?"

"Yep."

She screwed up her face as if working something out. "Mmm. Home to Lutton Ash. We'll hammer them even if we're down to five and blindfolded. OK, I'll let you off."

"Thanks." I laughed.

"My mum wants me to go in for that exam thing next year," Petra said as we jogged past the back of the away goal.

"Really?" I replied. "That would be great."

"No it wouldn't. I'm going to Mowborough High with Megan."

"You'd better!" Megan told her. "I'm not going on my own. That place is ginormous."

Lucy leaned forward. "You wouldn't be on your own. I'm starting there this September. So's Eve and Nika and Holly. We'll watch out for you next year."

"Hey! That's nearly all the Parrs!" Eve observed. She dug an elbow into my ribs. "Why don't you come, too, instead of going to that boring old Saggy Aggies?"

"Why do you want to go to that dump, anyway?" Jenny-Jane asked in that blunt way she has. "They look right weird in that uniform. Striped blazers. Who wears striped blazers?!"

There was a long gap as everyone waited for a response – but I didn't know what to say. This was exactly why I needed Amy here, so she could come out with something funny or sarcastic and draw attention away from me.

Instead it was Hannah who saved me. "OK, girls.

Let's have some shooting practice," she called.

"Me first!" Eve cried and charged forward.
Everyone followed.

For the next ten minutes we concentrated so hard
that conversation fizzled out and then it was time for
the match to start. My heart began pumping, all else
forgotten. This was what I loved. Hearing the whistle
blow and watching the ball, waiting for the sound
it makes when it connects with someone's boot.
That first touch. And then the play: the chasing,
the chances, the surge of power and energy that
courses through your whole body as you turn and
leave a defender standing. Nothing else I did, at
home or at school, came near to the exhilaration
I felt playing football.

Hannah put me in my usual central midfield spot
with Jenny-Jane on my right and Tabinda on my left
and Eve up front. "OK," Hannah said as we huddled
round. "This is the toughest, most testing part of
the season, when it's cold and miserable and the
pitches are in poor condition and it—"

"Snows," Megan said as a huge snowflake landed on her nose.

Everyone looked up at the sky. It was like a thick grey duvet waiting to burst.

"Nah! That's not snow; it's dandruff," Katie said, making us laugh.

Hannah clapped her hands together as the referee, one of the Tigers coaches, motioned to show he was ready. "Come on, Parrs. Let's have a good game!" she ordered.

# 4

**We had a very good game for about fifteen minutes.** Jenny-Jane held the right wing, sending some great crosses into the area for Eve and me. Eve scored twice from those. She scored a third after we'd made a run from deep in our half, passing the ball back and forth between the two of us until we were in front of the goal and all she needed to do was tap it in. "The Dream Team strikes again!" she yelled as she gave me such a forceful high five my hand tingled for ages afterwards.

I scored twice. The first was from the halfway line and the second was from a header. From then on the game became a bit one-sided as we were allowed most of the possession. After shaking off two of their defenders I heard one say to the other, "I hate her. She's too good." I wasn't at all – it was just that they gave in too easily. But after that I held back a bit, so I wouldn't draw more attention to myself. It made the game a bit boring, to be honest. I thrived in matches where I felt challenged, like when we played Grove Belles or the Vixens. "Come on, you lot! Liven up!" the Tigers coach kept calling out to them.

The only thing that livened up was the snow. It was falling more heavily now, swirling around us as if joining in with the action. Soon it became difficult to see; flakes kept landing on my eyelashes and I had to blink them away every few seconds. The whiteness was dazzling, and eventually the referee blew his whistle and held his arm up for us to stop play. "A word with the coaches, please," he said.

"I don't see what he's stopped the game for," Jenny-Jane complained as we waited to see what was happening. "I was enjoying that."

"I think it's something to do with us not being able to see the ball, doofus," Megan told her, pulling off the bandana she always wore and wringing it out.

"What happens if it's called off?" Petra asked.

"We go home and eat biscuits," Lucy said.

"What about the five goals, though? Don't they count?"

"Nope. We have to replay the match from scratch another time."

"That's not fair," Petra grumbled.


Fair or not, that's what happened.

"Sorry, girls, match abandoned," Hannah said. "That snow means business…"

"And there's no business like snow business!" Eve quipped.

"Into the changing rooms, quick," Hannah said, ushering us inside. "Get wrapped up and if anyone needs to borrow my mobile to call their parents let me know. I'll be next door in the communal area with Katie. Nobody leaves alone, OK?"

Eve and I weren't worried at first. We stayed in the changing rooms and chatted about the match, but after a quarter of an hour, when Mrs Akboh still hadn't arrived, we joined Hannah and Katie. They were sitting around a small wooden table, feet up, cups of coffee in their hands, chatting with the Tigers coaches. They all stopped when they saw us and smiled.

"Speak of the devil," Hannah said, looking straight at me. "We were just talking about you."

My heart sank. I hate it when people say things like that. I'd be happy to go through life with nobody ever talking about me at all.

The Tigers coach grinned at me. "One question, Gemma. Are you Marta in disguise?"

"Sorry?"

"Kayleigh thinks you're as ace as Marta, FIFA's Player of the Year," Hannah explained. "She reckons even in a snowstorm your talent shines through."

I glanced at the coach and gave her a polite smile.

"Yep. There's definitely a touch of class about you, Gemma Hurst," Kayleigh said. "Where does that come from? Mum? Dad?"

"Nowhere," I said, my skin prickling.

The other coach, who'd been the referee, took a slurp of his coffee. "Maybe she's related to Geoff Hurst!" he suggested.

Kayleigh laughed. "Shaun, she's not going to know who Geoff Hurst is."

He winked at me. "Don't patronize her. I bet she does."

He was right. I knew exactly who Sir Geoff Hurst was. He's best known for scoring a hat-trick in the 1966 World Cup Final against Germany, but he's also one of West Ham's all-time greatest players. Not that I would ever admit I knew that. This conversation was heading in a dangerous direction and I could feel myself shutting down inside. Again I wished Amy was with me. How wrong she'd been about me not needing her today! I glanced at Eve, desperate for her to say something instead.

She did the next best thing. Her mobile's ringtone belted out to the tune of *Jingle Bells*, making everyone laugh and giving me an excuse to disappear.

"I'm just going to the loo," I said as she answered it.

I stayed in the toilets for as long as I could, hoping that by the time I came out Mrs Akboh would be waiting for us and I could go home. No such luck. I returned to find everyone fussing around Eve and looking concerned.

"My mum's broken down on the motorway," Eve said, her eyes brimming with tears and her bottom lip quivering. "She's on her own and it will be at least an hour before the AA get to her because of the snow."

"Your mum'll be fine," Hannah reassured her. "They'll give her priority."

"Will they?" Eve asked, sounding doubtful.

"Absolutely. Lone women drivers always get priority."

Katie backed her up. "It's true."

Eve wiped her eyes with the back of her hand. "Good, because I'm one parent down already. I can't lose another." (Eve's dad died when she was little.)

Hannah gave her a brief hug. "Hey, don't say that, you muppet! Your mum's not in any danger. She'll be home before you know it."

"Definitely," I said, wanting to help.

"Trouble is we've got to lock up," Shaun told us, glancing at his watch.

"And we're supposed to be going to see friends in Manchester," Katie moaned, frowning at the snow swirling outside.

"Er… Well … I could call my mum and ask her to come and get us," I suggested.

That cheered Eve up. "She did say that, didn't she?"

"Yes, she did," I replied. Not that she expected us to take her up on it.

"Here, use my mobile," Eve said, thrusting her phone under my nose before I had a chance to reach for mine. "The Dream Team helping each other out in emergencies." She stood over me as I laboriously punched in Mum's number. "What will we do for two hours? Will I be allowed to sell kitchens?" she asked, breathing over my shoulder.

"No way," I said, trying not to think how Mum was going to react as I concentrated on the unfamiliar keypad. "We'll probably have to stay in the staff room."

"I don't mind."

"If you need a lift to the shop I can take you. I'm passing the shopping centre on the way," Katie offered just as Mum answered. I nodded gratefully. At least Mum wouldn't have to leave the shop, so that was one less thing to worry about.

"No need," Mum said when I explained what had happened. "Dad's just dropped some stuff off for me about five minutes from Cuddlethorpe. He'll come there and get you."

My head felt as if a dozen fire bells had been triggered inside it. "Dad? Isn't he *fishing*?" I asked, far too loudly.

"No, he isn't," Mum replied, trying not to sound exasperated with me and failing. "So he will pick you up and take you both straight home."

The alarm bells were deafening now and sending my pulse racing. Being with Eve in the shop was one thing. Being with Eve at *my* house, with *my* dad, was a different ball game altogether. "It's OK; Katie's passing right by…"

"Dad will pick you up and take you both straight home," Mum repeated firmly. She broke off to pass instructions to someone and then came back to the phone. "Gemma?"

"Yes."

"I need to hang up now so I can call him."

"Please don't," I begged, wishing I'd made the call on my own phone and in the privacy of the changing rooms. "Let us come to the shop. We'll be…"

"No, Gemma. I'm swamped here and who knows what the weather will be like in another hour. Eve's much better off waiting at home with you."

I lowered my voice so the others wouldn't hear the desperation in it. "Mum…"

She sighed and her tone softened. "This was bound to happen at some stage, honey. It's for the best, trust me."

"But, Mum…" Waves of panic were breaking over me.

"I'm sure nobody will recognize him," she continued. "The dreadlocks throw people every time."

"Not every time," I muttered, remembering the two guys who'd stopped us in Bluewater at Christmas.

Her tough-love voice returned. "It's non-negotiable, Gemma. I'm sorry," she said, and hung up.

I handed Eve her phone back.

"You OK?" she asked, looking at me curiously.

The fire bells gave one last, pathetic clang and stopped, knowing to continue was pointless. "Yes," I fibbed.

"So … am I giving you two a lift?" Katie asked.

I cleared my throat and attempted a smile that I'm sure looked more like a grimace. "No," I said.

"It's OK. My … my dad's on his way." I blinked in disbelief that those words had just left my mouth.

# 5

**I guess by now you think I'm deeply strange.** What's the big deal about having a friend back to your house, right? I mean, ten-year-olds do that all the time, don't they? It's not as if my dad's an axe murderer or anything, and it's not as if Eve's one, either. I know all that. It's just the two of them together ... this was not good. Not good at all. Unless I could stall Eve somehow, or at least steer the conversation away from fishing and football... I swallowed. The thought of me steering a conversation anywhere was a joke.

And what seemed like five seconds after the phone call, Dad pulled up in the SUV and honked his horn.

"Is that him?" Eve squealed, standing on tiptoes, so she could get a better view through the window.

"Woah!" she cried when I nodded. "Monster trucks!"

Dad turned round as I got in the car. Our eyes locked for a second. "All right?" he asked.

"Not really," I replied.

He tried to give me a reassuring smile as if to say "it'll be fine".

One thing I knew for sure: this would not be fine.

Dad turned to Eve then. She'd just climbed in, after barely waving to Hannah and Katie. He beamed at her. "Hey! I'm guessing you're Eve? How're you doing?"

I tensed, waiting for Eve to start her barrage of questions, but amazingly she only managed a brief "I'm good, thank you," that even I had to strain to hear. In fact, that's the most she managed for much of the journey. I'd never known her so quiet. It unnerved me more than her constant chattering. When Dad stopped talking to concentrate on the road, I tried to fill in the silence with my own pathetic questions such as "It's annoying about the snow, isn't it?" (yes) and "What's your favourite colour?" (orange). Really lame stuff.

It wasn't until we reached Toft's Hill that my team-mate found her voice. "They call this Toff's Hill near us," she announced when she read the street sign.

"Yes, I know," I replied. I'd been teased about it at school enough, even by girls with bigger houses than ours.

"Is it true that everyone who lives up here is a millionaire?" she asked me, her eyes flicking to the back of my dad's head.

"No." I sighed. I'd heard that one, too.

Dad chimed in. "Not everyone," he told her. "The Russian guy at number three's a billionaire."

"No way!" Eve gushed.

"Straight up," Dad said, thinking he was being funny.

"Don't listen to him," I snapped. "He's just winding you up."

"Oh," she said and broke into a grin. "I knew that!"

"There's not a castle on Castle Heights, either. It was just named after a family called Castle," I added, wishing my voice didn't sound so brittle, but the nearer we got to the house, the more tense I was becoming – if such a thing were possible.

"Got you," Eve said. She gazed out of the window. "But the houses look like mini castles," she added in a hushed voice when we turned into the complex. Her head was swivelling from side to side as she took in the snow-topped walls and security fencing that surrounded each property. "Even your gate's like a portcullis."

It was a fair point.

Inside, it was easier getting Eve upstairs and out of Dad's way than I'd thought it would be. It turned out she'd always wondered what my bedroom was like. She started at my dressing table, then moved across to my bedside cabinet, not trying one bit to hide how curious she was about my things. In the end she must have seen every corner of my bedroom, from the revision books on my desk to the clothes in my wardrobe, to the posters on my wall.

I didn't really mind. Having Eve upstairs was way preferable to having her downstairs. "I didn't know you were into astronomy," she said, striding over to the telescope by my window.

"Er… Yeah," I replied as she ducked to squint through the lens.

"How come it's trained on the gates and not the stars?"

"Dunno. Must have knocked it out of position."

"Oh."

I braced myself for more questions, but she'd lost interest and bounded across the floor. "What's in here? More clothes?" she asked, pushing open the door to my en suite. She gasped. "Oh! You've got your own bathroom!"

"Yes. It's only small…"

"*Small?* There's a shower and everything!" She disappeared inside. "Oh, I would give anything for my own bathroom. Or one I just share with

Mum. Do you know how disgusting boys are in bathrooms?" She peeked into my bathroom cabinet, sniffed my cocoa butter hand lotion and then turned to look at me. "You are so lucky."

"I know," I replied.

Eve returned for another snoop around my desk, then cast her eyes around the whole room. "Where are all your trophies?"

"What?"

"Your football trophies?"

I hadn't seen that one coming. "I … er … I don't put them out."

"What? Why?"

"They get too dusty."

"But you won Coaches' Player of the Season. Dust wouldn't dare gather on that."

"Well, it does."

She frowned. "It wouldn't in my house. Me and Mr Sheen would be on the case." She paused. "Couldn't your servants polish them?"

"We don't have servants!" I gasped.

"Whatever." She shrugged and then asked if she could look in my en suite again.

"Help yourself."

When she disappeared I glanced at my bedside clock. Please come quick, Mrs Akboh, I thought.

She didn't. By the time Dad called upstairs to tell us lunch was ready, I was sure Eve could have recited all of my possessions off by heart, in alphabetical order. If I hadn't been so on edge, I'd have found it funny.

"I'll go fetch the food," I said. "You can play on my Nintendo if you like."

I should have guessed she'd decline. "No, I'll come with you. I want to see what a real Hurst's Modern Kitchen of Mowborough kitchen is like!"

"OK." I sighed. "But please don't talk football with Dad," I added as though it was an afterthought. "He gets bored."

"No problem. I'll stick to fishing."

"Don't mention that, either."

"O-kaaay. Have you got a list of stuff I *can* talk about anywhere?"

I forced a smile. "Oh, Eve. You crack me up!"

"I get that a lot." She grinned.

# 6

In the kitchen, Caspar and Jake were eager to make friends with our unexpected visitor, pawing at her knees so she'd pay them attention. "Oh, they're so sweet," she said. "I want a dog, but Mum won't let me because we're out all day."

"That makes sense," Dad said, dishing hot tomato soup into beakers for us.

"Who looks after them when you're at work, Mr Hurst?" Eve asked.

"Call me Kriss," Dad told her.

"Thanks; I will!" Eve replied warmly.

"I don't go out to work," Dad told her. "This is my work. I am a housewife or househusband or lazy geezer, depending on which way you look at it."

"Really? Have you never had a proper job?"

"Ouch!" Dad laughed and pretended to pull a knife from his heart.

"Was I being cheeky?" Eve asked, tugging nervously at her earlobe. "Mum says I am without knowing it half the time."

"You're fine, Eve. I can take it," Dad reassured her.

"Have a sandwich," I said, sliding the bread mountain Dad had made towards her.

"And behave," she chided herself, going for the cheese and pickle.

"'Behave'? Hey, Eve, chill. This isn't school, you know," Dad told her.

"I know that! It's way too posh here to be my school."

I winced. I wished she would stop going on about how "posh" we were. It's not like she lived in a hovel.

"Good. Glad that's sorted. So how was the match?" Dad asked.

I caught my breath. What did he have to ask that for?

"It was OK until the snow ruined everything," Eve moaned.

"Have another cheese-and-pickle," I said, chucking a sandwich on top of Eve's plate. "Hey, do you want to help me revise after lunch?"

She nodded, and I congratulated myself on my quick thinking. Revision! Of course! It wasn't even an excuse. I really did need to revise. But my relief was short-lived.

"I scored a hat-trick," Eve told my dad.

"Yeah? Nice one," Dad replied. "How many's that so far this season?"

"Fifteen."

"Already? Impressive."

"Gemma's not far behind; she's on thirteen."

I gawped at her. What part of "no football" didn't she understand?

"Thirteen?" Dad repeated.

"Uh-huh."

He looked across at me, waiting for an explanation he had no chance of getting. "That's amazing for a sub..." he said, a note of puzzlement creeping into his voice.

I jumped up, hoping Eve would follow my lead – but I couldn't catch her attention.

"A sub? Gemma?" she said. "No way, dude! She's our star player. Even the opposition coach asked if she was Marta in disguise today."

I swear the floor tiles cracked beneath my feet at that moment.

"Marta? The Brazilian player?" Dad asked. Confusion had replaced puzzlement in his voice, and I was beginning to shake as if there was a real earthquake taking place in the kitchen.

"Eve..." I said, but my voice was nothing more than a squeak and she didn't hear. She just kept blathering on, making things worse and worse.

"Marta. Yep, she's that good," Eve told him. "As you'd know if you came to watch her now and again instead of going fishing!"

Oh no. "Eve..." invisible me pleaded again.

"I mean, choosing fishing over watching the

Coaches' Player of the Season play football. What's that about?"

Oh no. Oh no. *Oh no.* Unaware of what she'd started, Eve ran her finger around the pickle juice on the edge of her plate as she waited for an answer – but dad was lost for words. When she saw his dazed expression she glanced across at me and her hand flew to her mouth. "Ooops! I just talked about everything you told me not to, didn't I? Sorry."

*Sorry?* It was way too late for sorry. The mousy voice scampered off into the distance and what came out next must have reverberated along the whole of Castle Heights. "Eve Akboh!" I screamed at her. "You are the biggest blabbermouth I've ever met and I hate you."

Bomb detonated, I turned and fled upstairs.

# 7

**Normal people would have left me to stew after an outburst like that, but Eve doesn't do normal.** She followed me upstairs, didn't even pretend to knock on my door but came straight in and plonked herself right down beside me on my bed. "Well, this isn't awkward," she said after a few moments of utter silence.

I just glared at the zigzag patterns on my rug.

"Shall I sing the Hurst's kitchen jingle?" she asked.

"No," I grunted.

There was another pause. "I knew I'd blow it," Eve said and let out a deep, juddering sigh.

I glanced sideways at her. She was staring ahead, her hands tucked under her armpits, her back rigid. "Look, Eve..." I began, trying to think of a way to explain why I'd reacted that way, but my head felt too spongy to muster anything. "Eve," I said finally, "It's not you; it's me." She didn't seem to hear. She just continued staring at the snow falling outside my window. "Really," I added.

After a while she snapped to. "It's OK. You don't have to make excuses for me. It's my own fault."

"It's not..."

"It is. I know you're like a seriously private person and inviting me here was a big deal for you, but I got carried away. You asked me not to talk about football but I didn't listen, did I?"

I shook my head. "No," I whispered.

"It was just that your dad seemed OK with it. He mentioned it first..."

"I know."

She shrugged. "But so what? I still shouldn't have gone on about it. Pastor Kouamo is always telling me we've got one mouth and two ears for a reason. Now I know why." She stood up. "I'd better leave you in peace."

I cleared my throat and stood up, too. "OK."

"Can I just ask you one thing first?"

"What's that?"

"Do you really hate me? Because new research shows that hating people can seriously damage your health. Your teeth fall out and everything. I read it in the paper."

Despite her making light of it, I knew Eve wanted a serious answer to her question and I cringed with embarrassment. "Of course I don't hate you. I'm so sorry for saying that. I like you loads. We're the Dream Team, right?"

"Cool," she said, looking around as if trying to drink everything in for one last time. "Do you think Kriss would mind taking me home? I figure by the time we get across town my mum might be back. And even if she isn't I've got my key."

A few minutes ago I'd have jumped at that suggestion, but now I just felt crummy. How could I let her go home to an empty house after how I'd behaved? I couldn't let her leave like this, thinking she was at fault for something that had nothing to do with her. What sort of team-mate does that?

A sensation I usually only had on the pitch gripped me; it was daring me, urging me on. I grabbed her hand. "I want to show you something."

"Is it another bathroom?"

"No, it's something else."

"Pity," she said. "I'm pretty jazzed about your bathrooms."

# 8

**We returned downstairs, calling by the kitchen on the way.** Dad looked up. "Everything OK?" he asked, worriedly.

"Yes," I said. "I thought I'd show Eve the den."

His eyes met mine and I gave him a watery smile. "Sure," he said, a catch in his voice. "Go ahead."

"We'll talk later?"

"I'd like that." He nodded.

Eve, who didn't have a clue just how momentous that exchange was, bent to give Caspar a pat.

"Come on," I said, leading her through the kitchen and down the stairs off the utility room.

"Is this where you keep your millions?" she joked as she followed me down.

"Indeed," I replied, no longer hypersensitive about

everything she said. "Mind the gold nuggets don't fall on your head."

Of course there weren't any gold nuggets, or gold anything, unless you counted the gilded trophies and shields in the display cabinet on the far wall, but Eve missed them and homed in on the retro jukebox fitted above the American-style soda bar in the other corner. "How funky is this!" she gushed, sliding along the red leatherette seat and gurning at her reflection in the chrome trim.

"Not half as funky as these," I said. From a cupboard above her I pulled down a small selection of scrapbooks and took a deep breath. "OK, Eve. You're always going on about how much you love the sports pages of newspapers. Check these out." I slid the top scrapbook towards her and opened a page at random. It showed a picture of two players rising for the ball. I tapped the black player. "Know who that is?"

"No."

"That's my dad," I said.

"No way!" She laughed. "No way."

"It is. I swear."

She pressed her nose up against the page until it was almost touching the clipping. "He looks so different."

"It's the flat stomach. And the hair."

"You're not kidding." She peered more closely at the photo of Dad's shorn, almost bald head connecting with the ball. Then she looked at me. Her eyes agog, she pointed to his shirt. "Gemma, that's a West Ham shirt he's wearing."

"I know. It was one of his clubs."

"He was that good?"

"Yes. He could have played for England."

"Don't lie!"

"He could. He was selected but ... but it didn't work out."

"So he must have been really, really famous?"

"Not really famous. Like Joe Cole or Carlos Tevez," I said to prevent her getting too carried away. "But he was pretty well known. People stopped him in the street and wanted his autograph. Things like that."

"Wow! And did you have a mansion and fifteen Ferraris?"

"No, but we were well off," I admitted. "The house in London had a swimming pool. When we sold it we had enough to buy this house and to put money into Hurst's Kitchens."

"A swimming pool? Dude! I wish I'd known you then. I love swimming."

"I was only little. I don't remember it much, really."

"So how come you ended up in boring old Mowborough? The most exciting thing that ever happens here is that the traffic lights change!"

"That's exactly why we're here," I told her. "The more famous Dad got, the less of a private life we had. And after…" I had been going to say "after what happened" – but I stopped myself. There was only so much I was willing to reveal in one day. What I'd told her so far was more than anyone in

Mowborough, apart from Amy, knew. "After a while,"
I continued instead, "we got tired of the paparazzi
following us everywhere. Jumping out of bushes
and pushing microphones in our faces. I hated it.
Lizzie was older and handled it better, but I became
really clingy and timid. I would cry every time we
had to go out of the house. Mum and Dad were
really worried about me."

For the second time that day Eve clamped her
hand over her mouth. "That's why you hate having
your photo taken!" she gasped.

"Uh-huh."

"Amy told me it was because you used to be a
child model."

I laughed. "As if!"

She shook her head. "This makes much more
sense. It must have been scary."

Scary? Try terrifying, I thought. I cleared my
throat. "So to cut a long story short, Dad packed the
football in and we moved to Mowborough. Not just
because of the traffic lights," I said, trying to make

Eve smile. "Mum's from here and still had family in the town: my grandma and grandad Hurst. Grandad founded Hurst's Kitchens and Mum built it up and took over when he retired."

Eve frowned. "So Hurst isn't your dad's name?"

"No. It's my mum's last name. My dad's is Merrin-Jones." I opened a page in the second scrapbook at random and pointed to a caption beneath one of the team shots.

"Oh yeah!" Eve paused. "So why aren't you Gemma Merrin-Jones, then?"

"My mum and dad aren't married. They're not into stuff like that."

Of all the things I'd told her so far, that seemed to surprise her the most. She managed a short "Oh."

"I'm so glad I have Mum's name," I said, more to myself than to Eve. "It's made it easier to stay in the background."

"And if your dad stays home all day it makes it easier still."

"He does go out," I said, not wanting her to think Dad was a prisoner. "It's just my football I keep him away from, really."

"Because you're worried that people will recognize him and it'll all kick off again?"

"Exactly."

"But I don't get why he doesn't know how skilled you are. Why haven't you told him?"

A lump came to my throat as I remembered the hurt expression on Dad's face earlier. "I didn't want to hurt his feelings. I figured that if he thought I was useless he wouldn't mind so much that I didn't want him to come and watch. You know what football-mad dads are like. They get so serious about it. You just have to listen to Holly's dad and Megan's—"

It didn't sound nearly so convincing when I said it out loud and I expected her to pick me up on it, but instead she had a sad, faraway expression on her face, and I realized she was thinking of her dad. "Oh! I'm sorry."

Her face cleared immediately. "Don't worry about me. I've got two big brothers; that's like a full dad." She cocked her head to one side. "One more question, though, before I go and pinch all your body lotions. If football's caused all these problems for you, why did you even start playing it?"

I broke into a grin. "Now that *is* your fault."

"Mine?"

"Uh-huh. You and your nagging."

"Nagging? Me? Never. Akbohs don't nag."

"Not much they don't. That time at after-school club when you went on about this girl called Megan and this girls' team she was getting together and how it would be such fun if me and Amy came, too. In the end Amy said, 'Let's go or she'll never shut up.'"

Eve laughed. "But I was right, wasn't I? It is fun?"

I nodded. "It's more than fun. It's—"

The tune of *Jingle Bells* cut me off before I could finish. "It's from Mum," Eve said and began to read out loud. "'Home safe and sound, honeybunch' – that's me – 'but car kaput. Can you ask Gemma's parents to order you a taxi?'" Eve wiggled her eyebrows. "Gemma, honeybunch, could you ask your dad to order me a taxi?"

Dad wouldn't hear of it. "No way," he said, unhooking his car keys. "Nothing's going to get up and down Toff's Hill in this weather apart from tanks like mine."

Eve beamed. "I was hoping you'd say that."

The journey to Eve's was so different from the one coming. Eve didn't stop asking Dad questions about his career, or telling him about mine, all the way to her house. This time it was Dad who was the stunned one. I didn't know which tore me up inside the most: the way his eyes kept darting towards mine for permission to reply every time Eve asked him a question about his career or the pride and astonishment in his voice when she told me about me. It made me realize for the first time how tangled up everything had become.

After we'd dropped Eve off, I told Dad everything: about me, about the Parrs, about the best matches and the worst matches, about winning the Coaches' Player of the Season. I was trembling when I got to that bit. I knew how much it would have meant to him and Mum to have been there with all the other parents. I remembered how I'd forced Amy to promise she wouldn't tell them I'd won it. Now, sitting in the car with him, my fibs all seemed childish and pointless.

The paparazzi had long since lost interest. Nobody had recognized my dad in Mowborough for years. It was time to move on.

"Dad," I said as we almost reached the summit of Toft's Hill. He had stopped to give way to an oncoming car.

"Uh-huh."

"I was wondering..." I hesitated. My throat felt prickly.

"You were wondering?"

"When we get home, will you go through the

scrapbooks with me? Talk me through your days with West Ham and everything?"

"I'd love to," he said.

"And would you ... would you like to come and watch me play next week?"

He stalled the car and had to yank the handbrake on to stop us rolling backwards. I took that as a yes.

# 9

**The snow fell and fell all over the weekend and the following few days.** Schools were closed and Toft's Hill became a ski slope. Mum couldn't get to work and Lizzie couldn't get to college. I didn't mind. It was fun being at home as a family for once and it meant I could have a proper discussion with Mum and Dad about the Parrs.

"Does this mean I don't have to pretend your dad's the world's keenest angler any more?" Mum asked.

"Yes," I said. "In front of Eve, anyway."

She stroked my head. "I'm glad you told her. That's a big step forward."

"I'm glad I told her, too."

Dad gave my Coaches' Player of the Season award a final polish. "There," he said. "You can put it on your windowsill instead of that stupid telescope."

"I can put it *next* to the stupid telescope," I replied. I wasn't ready to let go of my lookout post just yet.

By Thursday the weather had eased. Temperatures rose, and while the fields and hills behind us remained wedding-cake white, the snow on roads and pavements had turned into that yucky sludge. Everything began moving again and we were told at school on Friday that the entrance exam would go ahead as planned.

I woke up on Saturday morning feeling much calmer than I'd expected. I even managed two warm croissants with apricot jam for breakfast. Afterwards, while I was upstairs brushing my teeth, Lizzie pressed her lucky keyring into my hand. "Pongy got me through my exams; he'll get you through yours," she told me.

I stared at the tiny koala bear in my palm and felt a little overwhelmed. For Lizzie to think my exam was as big as hers was mega. "Thanks, Lizzie,"

I said, trying not to drip toothpaste foam on him. "He's cute."

"Any time, sis," she said, pulling on her thick winter jacket as she prepared to catch the bus into town. Mum and Dad were both coming with me to St Agatha's, so she had to make her own way to Hurst's. "Hang on to him as long as you like."

"Cheers," I told her.

Downstairs, Mum and Dad were both pacing.

"All set?" Mum asked.

"All set," I said.

They didn't talk a lot during the journey. I think they were more nervous than I was.

"I wish I hadn't given up smoking for New Year," Mum muttered as we approached the grounds.

"Same here. What is this? Strangeways?" Dad said, eyeing the high wall that surrounded the school.

I smiled, remembering Jenny-Jane's indignant face when she'd asked why I wanted to go to St Agatha's. Well, this was why. Not the weird blazer or the grades or the facilities but the solid stone wall surrounding it. It was protection.

Amy and her mum, Debbie, were waiting in the car park. Mum, Debbie and Dad pecked each other on the cheek and Amy grabbed my arm. "I am so glad you're here. There are way too many Hermione Granger types around," she declared, scowling at a girl whose dark curly hair bounced as she walked.

"You'll be amazing," I told her. "I know you will."

Debbie squeezed my shoulder. "Thank you, sweetie. That's what I've been telling her all morning, but she's got the collywobbles."

"Really?" I stared at Amy in disbelief. She did look pale.

"I'd rather be playing Lutton Ash," she confessed.

"See what I mean?" Debbie asked. "She's *that* bad."

"Come on," I said, linking arms with my closest friend and looking after her for once. "This is going to be a breeze."

Together, we marched in through the main

entrance of St Agatha's school, and three hours later, we marched out again, bumping shoulders with the other hundred or so girls who'd taken the exam. Amy's collywobbles had disappeared. I knew because she did nothing but complain. "Not one question on compound words," she chuntered as we skipped down the steps. "Not one."

"Never mind. I bet you'll still have passed, even without them."

"'With-out.' Compound word."

"Foot-ball. Another one. I wonder what the score was."

She rolled her eyes. "Give it a rest, Hurst."

Across the grounds I could see Dad straining his neck to pick us out in the crowd.

"I can't." I grinned. "It's in the blood."

# 10

**On Monday, Eve pounced on us before we'd even got through the door of after-school club.** "How was it? How was it? How was it?" she trumpeted as Amy and I struggled to unload bags and coats and sandwich boxes in the titchy cloakroom.

"You mean the exam? It was OK," I said. "Better than we expected. How was the match?"

Eve plonked herself down on the bench opposite us. "Postponed. Waterlogged pitch."

"What? That's two in a row."

"Tell me about it," she groaned.

"What's two in a row?" Amy asked, half listening while she foraged in her bag for her pile of magazines. She was planning to catch up on lost reading time.

"Unplayed games. Lutton Ash was called off and Cuddlethorpe was abandoned because of the snow."

"Oh," Amy mumbled, arranging her magazines in order. She couldn't have been less interested.

Eve beamed. "It can snow every week if it means I can spend another afternoon at your house."

"'Scuse me? What?" Amy asked, suddenly all ears.

"Eve came to my house when the match was abandoned. Her mum's car broke down," I explained briefly. I hadn't had a chance to tell her about that Saturday yet. Well, I had – but I'd been postponing it because I knew how she'd react.

"Hey, did you find your trophies?" Eve asked, not noticing Amy's eyebrows getting higher and higher.

"Yes, they were in my toy box."

"Did you polish them?"

"Well, Dad did but I helped by telling him which bits he'd missed!"

"'Scuse me? What?" Amy asked again. Not

only were her eyebrows in danger of disappearing altogether but she had dropped all her magazines.

"Aw. I loved your dad. He was ace," Eve continued blithely. "And my mum was really grateful that Kriss took me home. She says she'll do the run this Saturday. The car's mended now."

"It's my mum's turn, isn't it?" Amy frowned.

Eve and I gawped at her. Amy never volunteered her mum if she could avoid it.

"It's OK. My mum feels bad for the Cuddlethorpe thing," Eve told her.

"Well, my mum does too," Amy countered.

I held up my arms to stop an argument developing. "Chill out! Nobody's mum has to do it. My dad and I have had a chat and..." I paused, took a deep breath and said, "he's going to pick up and drop off until the end of the season."

"Really?" Eve said. "Kriss Merrin-Jones is going to take us to football?"

"Really. So there's no need for the rota any more."

Eve leapt off the bench as if she'd been fired from

a gun. "That is *so* cool. High five, pard'ner."

"High five!"

Eve headed towards the club door. "See you both inside. I'm decorating cupcakes – come and help me when you're ready."

"Sure," Amy said, closing the door quietly but firmly behind her. She leaned against it, her arms folded, her foot tapping. "'Scuse me, 'pard'ner', but what in the name of Lindsay Lohan's leggings is going on?"

I sighed and explained what had happened as briefly as I could.

"You told her? Everything?!" Amy asked.

"Not everything. I didn't tell her about ... you know."

"I should think not," Amy replied, looking genuinely shocked. "But she knows who your dad is? Who he played for and everything?"

"Yes."

"And Kriss knows you're a hotshot superstar who makes everybody else look feeble?"

"He knows I can play a bit," I corrected.

There was a moment's pause while Amy let that register. Then she bent to pick up her magazines. "Fine. It's your life. I just hope you're ready for the fallout."

"There won't be any fallout."

"No, Gemma. Course not." She stood up and strode towards the door, pushed it open with her elbow and was gone. I stood there for a moment, frowning as the tiniest seed of doubt began to grow.

# 11

**The seed of doubt grew some more on Saturday morning.** I was soon having kittens about Dad taking me. Amy was right. Even if Eve didn't blab, people were bound to ask questions. I mean, he'd been like the Invisible Man for a year and a half. I'd never even talked about him. How would I explain his sudden appearance?

"Easy. Just tell them he jacked-in fishing," Amy suggested when I admitted I needed her help. "And tell him to come up with an excuse why he's given up, too."

So Dad had been primed to say that he'd given up fishing because Mum was so busy in the shop she needed him to help out. It sounded reasonable. "You could have given me a hobby I knew something about," he had grumbled.

When we arrived at the ground, Dad melted away into the background, going to stand on the other side of the pitch.

"Why doesn't he go over to..." Eve began, saw my expression and pulled a pretend zip across her lips.

I needn't have worried about the team. Megan and the others greeted the three of us like they always did. Petra asked us about the exam, but most of the pre-match conversation was about Hixton Lees. "They're doing all right in the league," Megan said in that earnest way she has; "so we need to watch them."

Good, I thought, hoping everyone would listen to her. If they were watching Hixton, it meant they wouldn't be watching Kriss Merrin-Jones.

As it turned out, the only one who seemed to be aware of my dad was me. I wasn't used to him or anyone from my family standing on the touchline and I found it hard to concentrate.

I missed a cross from Nika and fluffed three really easy chances on goal. Luckily, Eve was around to cover my back. She was playing a blinder – falling back in defence, helping out in midfield, charging down the Hixton goalie every time she had a goal kick. Once or twice she was even a little greedy and didn't pass to Nika when Nika was in a better position to shoot. But still, it was miraculous that we ended the first half without scoring.

"Someone's had their Weetabix." Hannah smiled at Eve when we walked off at half-time.

"Coco Pops, actually." She grinned.

"You all right, Gemma?" Hannah asked me. "Only you seem a little distracted."

"No," I said, glancing over my shoulder at Dad and wondering whether I ought to go over and talk to him or stay with the team. He was chatting to Holly and Nika's parents, but put his thumb up at me when he saw me looking. "No, I'm fine."

☆ ☆ ☆

In the second half I began to play a little better. Nobody on the team had said anything and my dad had somehow blended in with the other parents, so I relaxed. I began to tune in to the game more, predicting where balls would go and how they would go. My interceptions became sharper and my ball control surer. I scored twice, once from outside the box with a full volley and once with a simple side-foot in that the keeper wasn't quick enough to stop.

"Nice one, mate!" Eve said, running to congratulate me.

A few minutes later I was doing the same to her as she neatly slid in a pass from me to put us three–nil up. "The Dream Team strikes again!" she declared.

Mid-table Hixton Lees didn't let us have it all our own way, though, and replied soon after with a zinger that caught out our defence. Game on!

I was enjoying it and could have played for ever, but Hannah pulled us both off midway through the half. "Better give the others a chance, eh?" She grinned, patting our backs as we made way for Jenny-Jane and Amy.

"Show-offs!" Amy said as I high-fived her.

"Shurrup!" I laughed.

Usually we hovered around the other resting team-mates when we weren't playing, but Eve shook her head when I asked if we should join Lucy and the others. "No. Let's go and talk to Kriss," she said and began haring around the perimeter of the field to where he was standing. I trotted after her, feeling a little strange and wondering what he'd say. It was all right for Hannah and everyone to big me up, but my dad had been a professional. He might think I was useless.

"Not bad," was what he said.

"Not bad? We're brilliant!" Eve told him and punched him in the arm.

I laughed and decided it was cool having my dad watching. Really cool. Why had I left it so long? I linked my arm through his. Eve, standing on the other side of him, saw me and did the same. I didn't mind a bit. He wouldn't have been there if it wasn't for her. I hadn't felt so happy in ages.

# 12

**The following Saturday we were playing Greenbow at Greenbow.**

"You'll like these guys, Kriss," Eve told my dad in the car. "They're good. And their coach has dreadlocks even longer than yours."

"Yeah?" Dad asked.

"Yeah," she continued, the top of her head just visible above the raised headrest. "But be careful where you park in the community centre. It's in a well dodgy area. Last time my brothers played here they had half their kit pinched from the minibus."

He already knows, I wanted to say. I told him this morning.

I was about to lean forward in my seat to hear better, but Amy pulled me so close towards her that I could smell the peppermint toothpaste on her breath. "Where will you put all your stuff?" she asked me in a low voice.

I glanced at her. "What do you mean?"

She pressed her lips together to stop herself from giggling. "When she moves in with you."

"Shut up!" I told her, digging my elbows into her ribs.

"OK, change of subject. Why is it taking so long to get our results? Mum's going to buy me a pair of boots if I pass and if I don't hear soon I know my size will have sold out. Happens every time."

"I don't know. Next week, maybe?" I shrugged and turned away. I didn't want to talk about St Agatha's. I wanted to talk about football with Dad and Eve. I leaned forward again, eager to join in but Amy interrupted me again, and again. In the end I gave up.

We arrived at the ground quite early, so Dad was able to find a parking spot right under the CCTV camera in the car park. "Nice," he said, glancing around at the boarded-up pub and dilapidated-looking community centre. "It reminds me of where I grew up. I hope the pitch is in better nick than the car park."

"It's not bad," I told him. "A bit bobbly."

"Hang on a tick," Amy said as Dad and Eve began walking towards the playing field.

I turned to see what she wanted.

"I need to do my hair," she explained.

"But it looks fine."

"It's not prepped," she replied. She ducked down to check out her ponytail in the wing mirror, decided it was a disaster and began retying it. Meanwhile, Eve and Dad had sauntered ahead.

"Come on," I told Amy as she began double-checking to see if her hairslides were even. "Hurry up."

"This is my routine. You know it is."

"I know but it's not important. The important part is playing."

I'd never done that before. Hurried her along. Told

her how annoying it was to wait for her to faff about with her hair and make-up. I'd always kept quiet, but that day I didn't have the patience. I wanted to chat to Dad and to be with Eve and the others, warming up, getting into the zone. Greenbow were good – they would give us a decent game. Amy, though, wouldn't be hurried. She'd produced a pot of lip gloss.

"Amy! Not the lip gloss!" I pleaded with her.

She put it on anyway, gave her ponytail one final tug and then got out her iPhone.

"Now what?" I groaned. In the far distance I could see Eve and Megan heading a ball to each other. This was agony.

"Oh, look! I've just had a Tweet," Amy said.

"What?"

"A Tweet, which says: 'Remind G that some people aren't here to play. Some people couldn't give two hoots about playing.'"

I snorted. "You can say that again."

She held up her hand. "Second Tweet alert:

'Some people are here because their friends used to need them around.'"

With that she began striding towards the field, her ponytail swishing back and forth like an angry teacher's finger telling me off. My chin wobbled. She was right. I was the reason she was here. I was the one who had persuaded her not to drop out of the Parrs after the first couple of weeks when it became painfully obvious that she found playing football only mildly preferable to being slapped by a wet fish. But she came anyway, for my sake, to be my bodyguard and my friend.

I chased after her and threaded my arm through hers. She didn't shrug me off. She never does. Amy's not one to sulk. "I still need you," I told her.

"I know you do, babes," she said, smiling good-naturedly. "I've seen inside your wardrobe."

# 13

**Despite the bad start with Amy and the day being grey and drizzly, the first half of that match against Greenbow was the best one of my life.** I loved every moment. Everything went right. I'm not talking about the three goals I scored – they were just the icing on the cake. I'm talking about the feeling I had when I tracked the ball. The adrenalin rush as my crosses found Eve or Nika nearly every time. The elation at evading the Greenbow defence – dancing around one, two, three of them as they tried to close me down. The buzz as Eve linked up with me and we passed the ball forward between us until one of us had a shot at goal. I was playing out of my skin, and for the first time I didn't care who knew it.

For once, Hannah didn't swap me midway through the half like she usually does so that everyone has a chance of a game. I glanced across at her when she took Eve off, but she just stuck her thumb in the air for me to "Carry on" and leaned over to whisper something to Katie.

On the other side of the pitch, Dad was standing slightly apart from the rest of the parents, watching me intently. Even while I was on the ball, fully focused, I was aware of him and I knew he was proud. I knew he thought I was more than "not bad" today, and that was what I wanted. To show him what I could do. To make up for all the times he'd missed.

When the whistle blew for half-time there was a moment's stillness. I walked towards the touchline, took a swig of water and tried to act normal, but my heart was bursting. I couldn't wait to go over to Dad, but Hannah crooked her finger at me, pulling me away from the others. I gave her a shy smile.

"We need to talk," she said.

"Sure," I told her.

But she didn't seem to know where to begin. I think she was trying to work out how not to scare me off, so that I wouldn't become uncomfortable with her like I usually am.

"I let go," I said, hoping that would help her out.

Hannah laughed then. "'You let go'? Yeah, just a bit! Gemma, you were beyond awesome..."

"Thank you."

"You know you've got a real talent, don't you?"

I nodded. It would have been churlish to deny it.

"And you know you mustn't waste it. You've got to go for trials next season, either with a big club that has a girls' academy or at the new centre of excellence."

"OK," I said.

Her eyes widened in surprise. "OK? Really?"

"Really."

"Well, that was easier than I thought it was going to be."

I shrugged. "I'm ... I'm ready now."

Hannah pinched my cheek. "You were born ready."

"What about Eve?" I asked, glancing around but not seeing her in the huddle. "Will she be able to come for trials, too?"

"Why not? We can't split up the Dream Team, can we?"

"No," I agreed; "we can't."

"Come on," she said, putting her arm around my shoulders; "let's get back to business."

# 14

**I wish I could tell you that was how it ended.** That I finished the season with the Parrs on a high, winning both the league and the cup, and that afterwards me, Eve and a few others had trials for the centre of excellence and we all got in. Oh, and that Amy and I aced the entrance exam, but Portia Poohsbreath failed and we all lived happily ever after.

I really, really wish I could tell you that. Only I can't. I can't even tell you that the euphoria lasted for days because it didn't – it didn't even last until the end of the match. Why? Eve Akboh, that's why.

After our conversation, Hannah and I walked back to the touchline for the start of the second half. Hannah made some changes. "OK, girls, just keep doing what you're doing. Let's see … Minto, you look perished. Warm up. I'm putting you on for Gemma."

"Me?" Amy said, shivering. "I can't. I've got terrible growing pains." She doubled over and started groaning.

Jenny-Jane spat an orange pip out of her mouth. "Forget her. She's a waste of space. Leave Gemma on. She's ripping 'em to shreds."

"Shut up, JJ! I am not a waste of space," Amy told her.

"Prove it," JJ retorted.

Hannah tutted. "OK, OK. I don't want any domestics! JJ, you're on for Gemma. Minto – get your growing pains under control. You're on in ten."

"If you insist," Amy replied and offered me a stick of gum.

"No, thanks," I said, "I want to go and talk to my dad."

"You'll be lucky."

I frowned. "What do you mean?"

She nodded across to where before half-time, Dad had been standing alone. Now there was a small crowd of five or six teenage boys around him. I recognized two of them as Eve's brothers, Claude and Samuel, but I didn't know the others. Eve was there, too, talking away ten to the dozen.

"Oh," I said, feeling deflated. Alarm bells didn't quite go off at that moment – Claude and Samuel did sometimes come to watch Eve play and occasionally some of their friends did too – but I'd so wanted to talk to Dad on his own.

"Do you want me to come with you?" Amy asked.

"Sure," I said.

We strode arm in arm around the perimeter of the field. I told Amy what Hannah had said. "That's cool, if that's what you want," she said. "Hey, if you get really good I could be your agent. I fancy myself as the next Karen Brady."

"You fancy yourself full stop," I told her.

"Oooh, cutting. I'm not so sure I'm liking this new sarcastic streak, girlfriend."

I started to giggle, but when we reached the huddle around my dad, I stopped, feeling self-conscious, especially as Eve looked so startled to see us.

"Oh!" she said. "Are we on again?"

"No, we're resting," I told her.

"And I'm growing," Amy added.

Sam and Claude turned to me, but the other boys continued chatting away to Dad.

"Hiya, Gem," Samuel greeted me, a broad smile on his face. "I hear you're on fire today."

"Hello," I said, loosening myself from Amy as I tried to edge my way to Dad. The three other boys seemed reluctant to let me through, but Dad noticed and sidestepped around them.

"OK, fellas," he said. "It was nice meeting you. I'm just going to talk to my daughter for a minute, OK?"

"Sure," one of the boys replied. "We've got to head off anyway. It was cool meeting you, Kriss."

The others nodded.

"Yeah."

"Really cool."

"Wicked, man."

I relaxed a little. Good. They were going. But one of them, a tall boy with his hoodie pulled tight around his face, stayed put. "Yo, Kriss. Before we go, is it OK to have a photo of you?"

I tensed and Dad automatically did too.

"No way, Marlon," I heard Eve say as she realized what was happening.

Amy went further. "Don't you dare!" she barked and made a grab for his camera.

"Butt out!" Marlon told her, trying to push her away. "It's no big deal."

"It is if you've been through what she's been through, you meathead!" Amy yelled at him.

But it was too late. The damage was done. Maybe if the flash hadn't gone off, I wouldn't have reacted so badly – but as soon as he pressed the button that was it. The light in my eyes, the scuffle all around me, the cries and the commotion were exactly, *exactly* like when I was four and being led out of that flat by the police and into the pack of photographers after the ransom had been paid.

# 15

**Yes, that's right. The ransom. That thing kidnappers ask for when they take someone against their will.** They're all the rage in the football world. Players' families are easy targets, even ones like mine who weren't in the superstar league.

I was lucky. My kidnappers only held me for two days and they didn't hurt me. They gave me sweets and toys to play with. They let me watch CBeebies because they knew it was my favourite. Funnily enough, that was how the police caught them afterwards. I hadn't told them I liked CBeebies; I hadn't told them anything. It was my nanny who'd given them that information when she'd helped set it up. My nanny. Isn't that awful? So now you have it. The real reason I'm so weird about people knowing about my private life and why I couldn't even fill in the player profile properly at the beginning of this story. The real reason my dad stays at home all day is so I know exactly where he is if I need him.

"I knew telling Eve was a mistake," Amy said the next day. She was pacing up and down my bedroom floor while I sat huddled on my bed. I was still in my pyjamas, even though it was late afternoon. "I knew she'd blab. As soon as I saw the gang go up to your dad at half-time, I thought, uh-oh, here we go…"

I rubbed a hand across my stomach. It ached. I hadn't eaten all day, but the thought of food made me feel sick. "It was the flash … if it hadn't flashed I'd have coped better, but everything came back…"

"Well, dur! It would for anyone who'd been kidnapped. It's called trauma. Just wait until we see Akboh at after-school club on Monday. Just wait."

"No, Amy. Don't say anything to her. Promise me."

"What?"

"Seriously. It'll only make things worse."

"So what are you going to do? Act like nothing happened?"

"Me? I'm not going to do anything. I won't be there."

Amy stopped pacing. "'Scuse me?"

I slid down from my bed and strode across to my telescope. I peered through it for the twentieth time that day, turning it first in one direction, then in another. "I'm not going to after-school club any more. I'm not going to football, either."

"What? Why?"

"Because those boys will have told their mates. Their mates will tell their parents. Their parents will know someone in the press..." I blinked as my view of the electronic gates went black until I realized Amy had put her hand over the lens. "Don't," I told her.

"Hey! I'm supposed to be the drama queen around here, not you, so stop it," she said. "And no offence, but even the *Mowborough Mercury* isn't going to turn up to cover a story about a girl who gets jumpy about having her photo taken."

I straightened up and returned to my bed. Mum, Dad and Lizzie had spent all day trying to convince me of the same thing. Dad had pleaded with me not to undo all the progress I'd made, but it was too late. I was back where I'd started, as jittery and clingy as ever. "Maybe you're right," I said to Amy. "But I'm still not going to after-school club and I'm not going to football."

"OK, I'll let you drop after-school club but you can't drop football. You love football. You're brilliant at it. Even I know that."

"Don't you see? That's the problem."

"What do you mean?"

"It means I get singled out. It means I get attention. 'Merrin-Jones kidnap girl to play for England.'"

"England? Get you!"

"I'm just thinking ahead to what *might* happen. Newspapers love that kind of stuff. They'll bring it up every time I'm interviewed and I just know I wouldn't be able to hack it." I frowned as something occurred to me for the first time. "Do you know what?"

"What?"

"Eve did me a favour. Telling her brothers about Dad gave me a peep into what I might have let myself in for if I'd joined a centre of excellence." I shuddered, remembering what I'd agreed with Hannah.

Amy opened her mouth to say something, changed her mind and shoved a letter under my nose instead.

"What's that?"

"I have no idea."

I couldn't help grinning at that. "Fibber. It's got the St Agatha's crest on it."

"Has it? I never noticed."

"Not much."

"It came yesterday," she admitted. "Mine, too."

I stared at the envelope. "I should wait for Mum and Dad."

"They kind of already know."

I glanced closer and realized that the flap was unstuck and slightly torn.

"They didn't want you even more upset – you know – in case…" Amy explained.

"So I've passed?"

"Uh-huh."

"And you did?"

She lifted her chin in the air. "Of course. My funky new boots are being dispatched as we speak."

I set the letter to one side. There wasn't much point opening it now. "Cool," I said, remembering the wall around the school. "Really cool."

# Final Whistle

OK, I'm going to bow out here. Sorry.
I know it's an abrupt way to end,
but I stopped going to football after
the Greenbow match, so there's not
much more I can tell you about what
happened after that. I did ask Megan
if she wanted me to get Amy to fill
in for me, so there wouldn't be a gap
in the Parrs' history, but she said
it was fine: Eve would do it. It was
her turn next on the rota apparently;
she'd just have to start a little
earlier, that was all.

Amy thought it was wrong for Eve to
take over when she'd caused so many
problems, but I don't see it that
way at all. I'm glad Eve is the one
following on from me. It feels right,
me passing to her just like I used
to on the pitch. After all, we're

still the dream team, right? And I
know Eve will make a brilliant job
of it; she's confident and comical
at the same time. I wish I could be
more like her. I'm more of a work in
progress.

Anyway, I'd better be off. I've
promised Dad I'll go with him when he
takes the dogs out for a run. From
the sounds of all the barking going
on downstairs that means NOW!

Wrap up warm,
Gemma xx